MARVEL
AVENGERS ASSEMBLE

BUILT FOR ACTION

adapted by **Bill Scollon**

studio fun BOOKS

White Plains, New York • Montréal, Québec • Bath, United Kingdom

It's a day made for flying. Iron Man and Arsenal, his robotic sidekick, zoom through the clouds. Arsenal mirrors Iron Man's every twist and turn. "There's no quit in you," laughs Tony Stark.

A transmission from Falcon interrupts the flight. "Grim Reaper's escaped. Are you guys ready to stop him, or are you trying out for *Dancing with the Super Heroes*?"

"Arsenal needs to stretch his legs," answers Tony. "He's my dad's greatest invention. His energy comes from the Power Stone socketed in his chest. He is a real masterpiece."

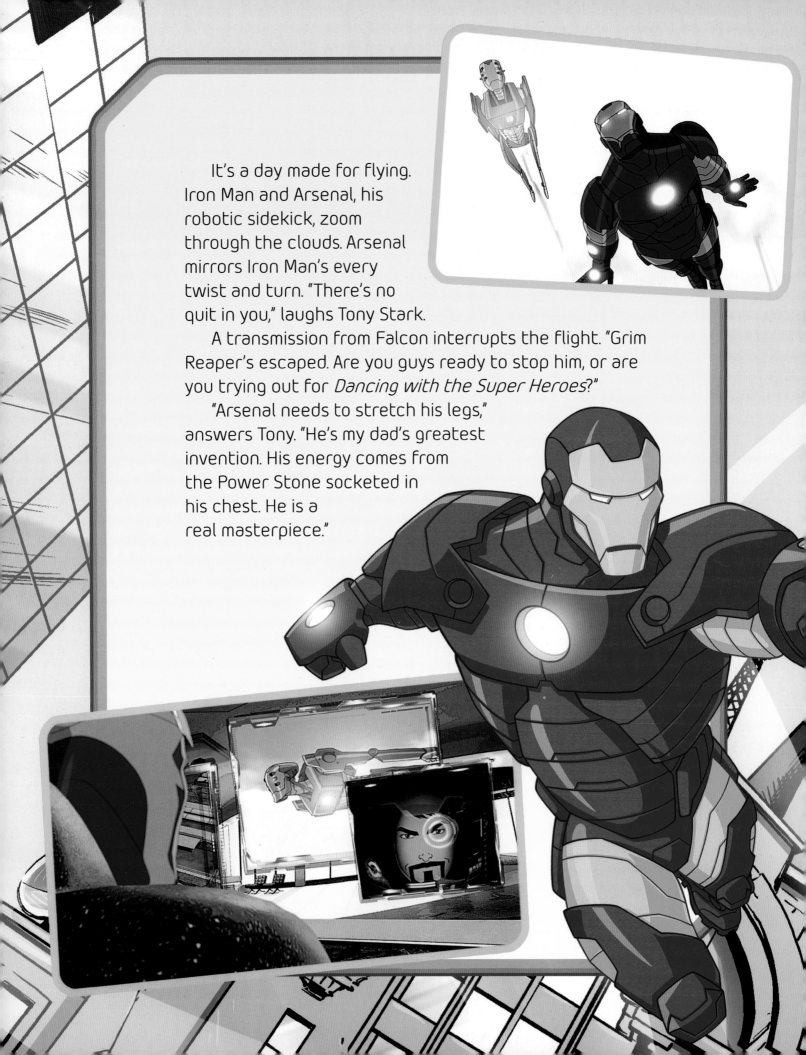

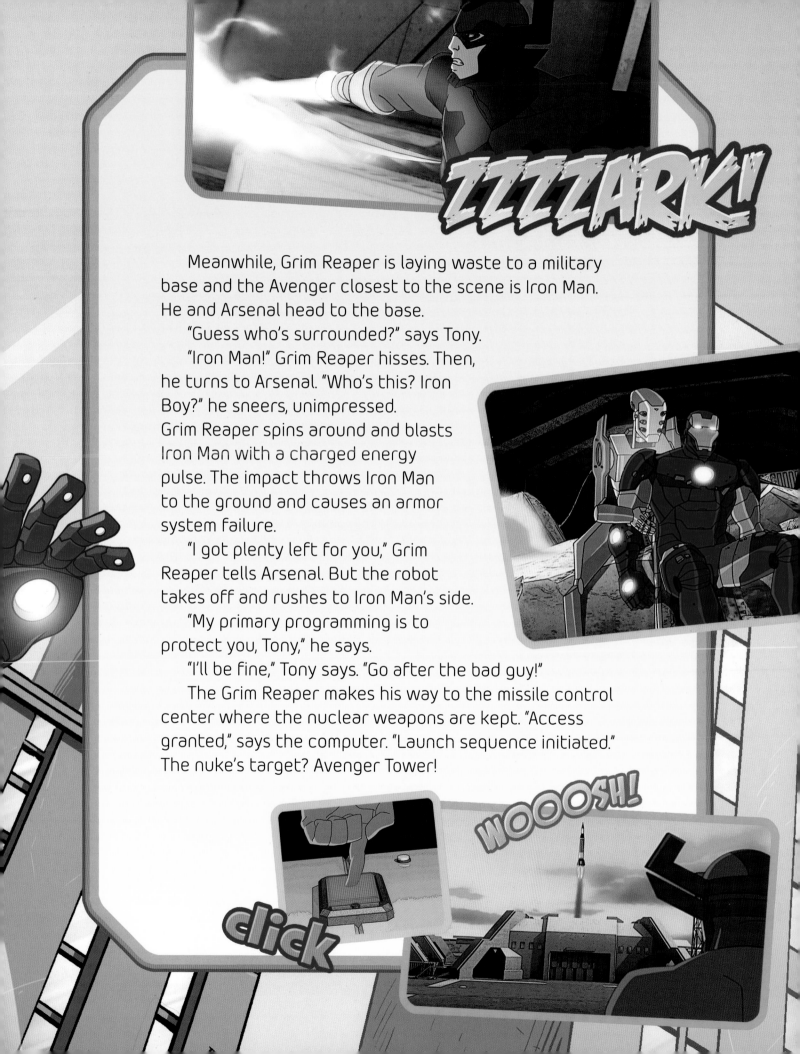

ZZZZARK!

Meanwhile, Grim Reaper is laying waste to a military base and the Avenger closest to the scene is Iron Man. He and Arsenal head to the base.

"Guess who's surrounded?" says Tony.

"Iron Man!" Grim Reaper hisses. Then, he turns to Arsenal. "Who's this? Iron Boy?" he sneers, unimpressed. Grim Reaper spins around and blasts Iron Man with a charged energy pulse. The impact throws Iron Man to the ground and causes an armor system failure.

"I got plenty left for you," Grim Reaper tells Arsenal. But the robot takes off and rushes to Iron Man's side.

"My primary programming is to protect you, Tony," he says.

"I'll be fine," Tony says. "Go after the bad guy!"

The Grim Reaper makes his way to the missile control center where the nuclear weapons are kept. "Access granted," says the computer. "Launch sequence initiated." The nuke's target? Avenger Tower!

click

WOOOSH!

The Avengers see the missile. "That rocket won't just take out the tower," warns Falcon. "It'll take out half of New York!"

Captain America calls for Thor. "We got a missile targeting Manhattan. Get here!"

"You cannot keep me from battle," comes the reply.

At the base, Iron Man orders Arsenal to intercept the missile.

Thor uses his hammer to divert the rocket. "I will throw it into the heart of the sun!"

But Falcon has bad news. The missile is designed to detonate if it changes course!

BOOM!

"Thor!" shouts Falcon.

"Energy contained," announces Arsenal. The robot has the ability to capture and store immense amounts of power. Thor lives!

CRACKLE! CRACKLE!

Grim Reaper can't believe what he sees on the screen. "That's impossible!"

Iron Man, fully rebooted, blasts him. "We're Avengers," he says. "We do impossible!"

With Grim Reaper out of commission, the Avengers assemble at the tower. Hawkeye is surprised to see Arsenal there. "He's an Avenger now? So can my coffee-maker join, too?"

"Stopping a 30-megaton missile's not impressive enough for you?" asks Tony.

"It is for me," says Hulk, turning to Arsenal. "I like you, robot."

Just then, Captain America receives a message from Director Fury. "Remind me not to let the Avengers visit my hometown," he says. "This city is ruined."

The Avengers had recently defeated an alien fleet there with little collateral damage. But the picture Fury puts up tells a different story.

Captain America has a pretty good idea who's responsible. "Thanos."

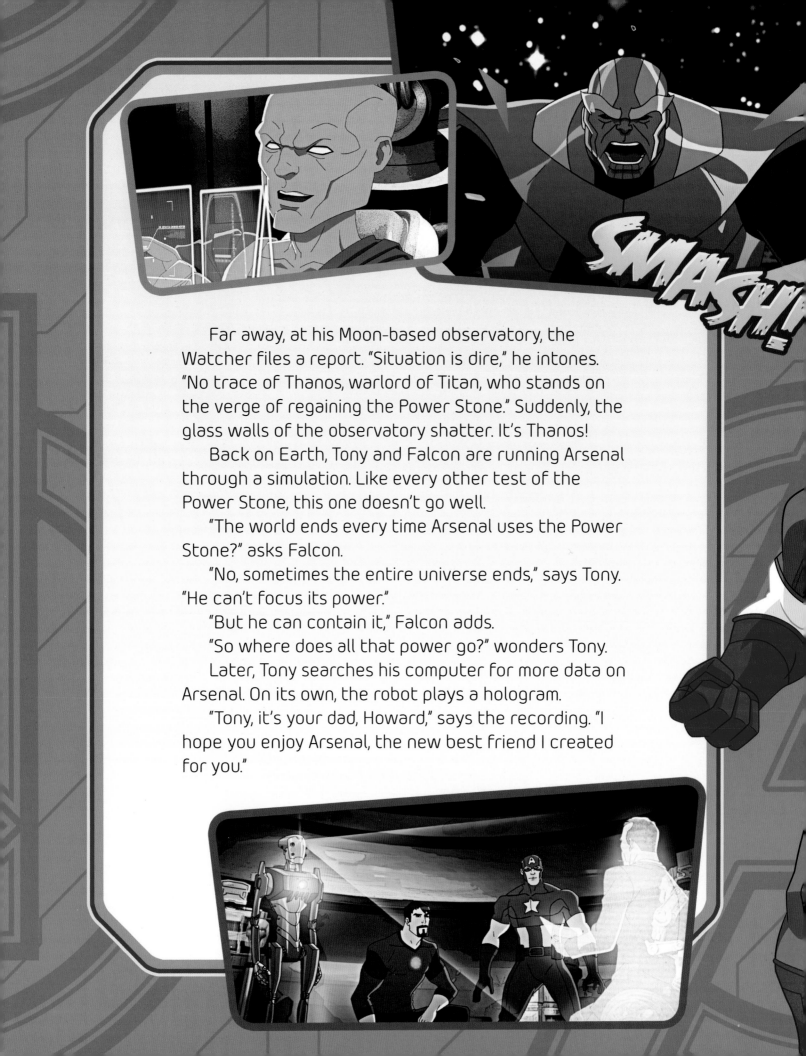

Far away, at his Moon-based observatory, the Watcher files a report. "Situation is dire," he intones. "No trace of Thanos, warlord of Titan, who stands on the verge of regaining the Power Stone." Suddenly, the glass walls of the observatory shatter. It's Thanos!

Back on Earth, Tony and Falcon are running Arsenal through a simulation. Like every other test of the Power Stone, this one doesn't go well.

"The world ends every time Arsenal uses the Power Stone?" asks Falcon.

"No, sometimes the entire universe ends," says Tony. "He can't focus its power."

"But he can contain it," Falcon adds.

"So where does all that power go?" wonders Tony.

Later, Tony searches his computer for more data on Arsenal. On its own, the robot plays a hologram.

"Tony, it's your dad, Howard," says the recording. "I hope you enjoy Arsenal, the new best friend I created for you."

There are 108 recordings of Tony's father stored inside Arsenal. One of them explains how Arsenal shuttles excess power into a parallel dimension. To protect Tony, Arsenal can bring the power back, but it would destroy the robot in the process.

Out of the blue, a meteor heads for the tower.

"Any of you expecting a high-velocity visitor?" yells Falcon.

The fireball smashes through the window. It's the Watcher! Thanos threw him off the Moon.

"It's an invitation," says Captain America.

"Couldn't he have just used e-mail?" asks Hawkeye.

"It's a trap," Black Widow warns.

"Trap or no trap," says Tony, "we've got some avenging to do."

FWOOM!

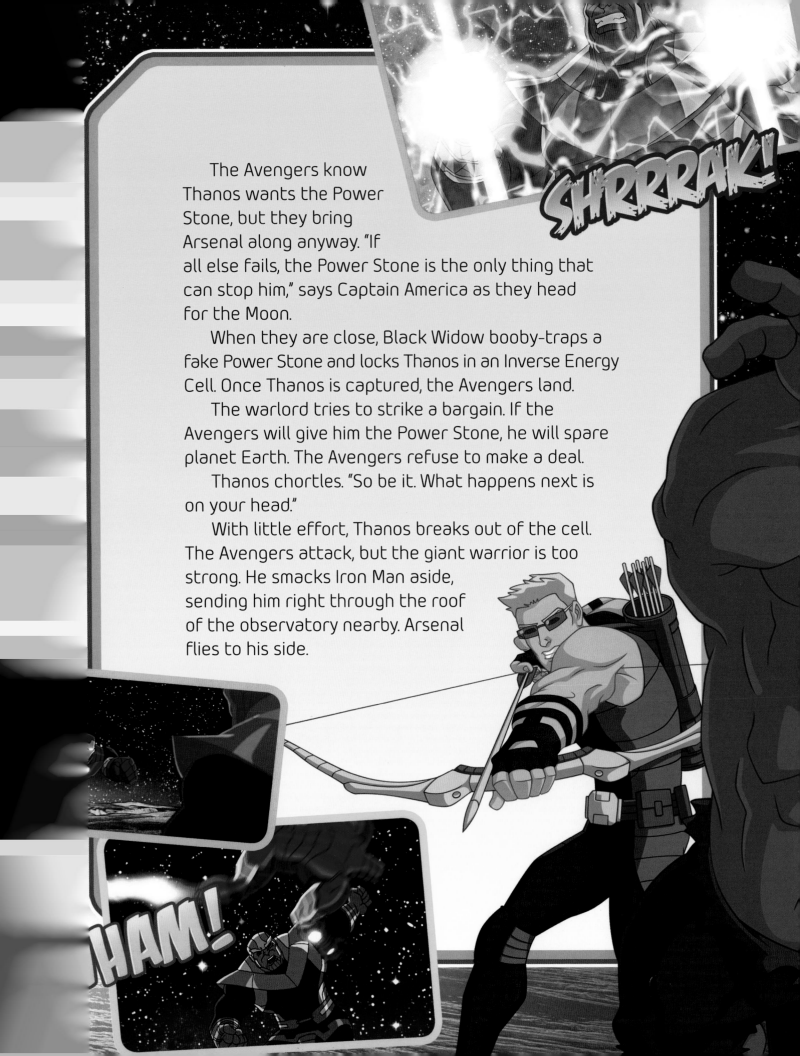

The Avengers know Thanos wants the Power Stone, but they bring Arsenal along anyway. "If all else fails, the Power Stone is the only thing that can stop him," says Captain America as they head for the Moon.

When they are close, Black Widow booby-traps a fake Power Stone and locks Thanos in an Inverse Energy Cell. Once Thanos is captured, the Avengers land.

The warlord tries to strike a bargain. If the Avengers will give him the Power Stone, he will spare planet Earth. The Avengers refuse to make a deal.

Thanos chortles. "So be it. What happens next is on your head."

With little effort, Thanos breaks out of the cell. The Avengers attack, but the giant warrior is too strong. He smacks Iron Man aside, sending him right through the roof of the observatory nearby. Arsenal flies to his side.

SHRRRAK!

HAM!

POW!

CLANG!

SMASH!

The Avengers attack. Captain America is knocked head over heels! Hawkeye's exploding arrows are useless. Even the incredible Hulk and Thor are no match for Thanos. The Avengers desperately need a better plan.

"Is it time for me to employ the Power Stone?" asks Arsenal. But Tony knows that if he does, he'll probably blow up the Moon! He needs to find a way for Arsenal to focus all that power. Tony's eyes go to the Watcher's amazing telescope.

"Uatu, old pal," Tony tells the Watcher. "I'm going to need to use some stuff."

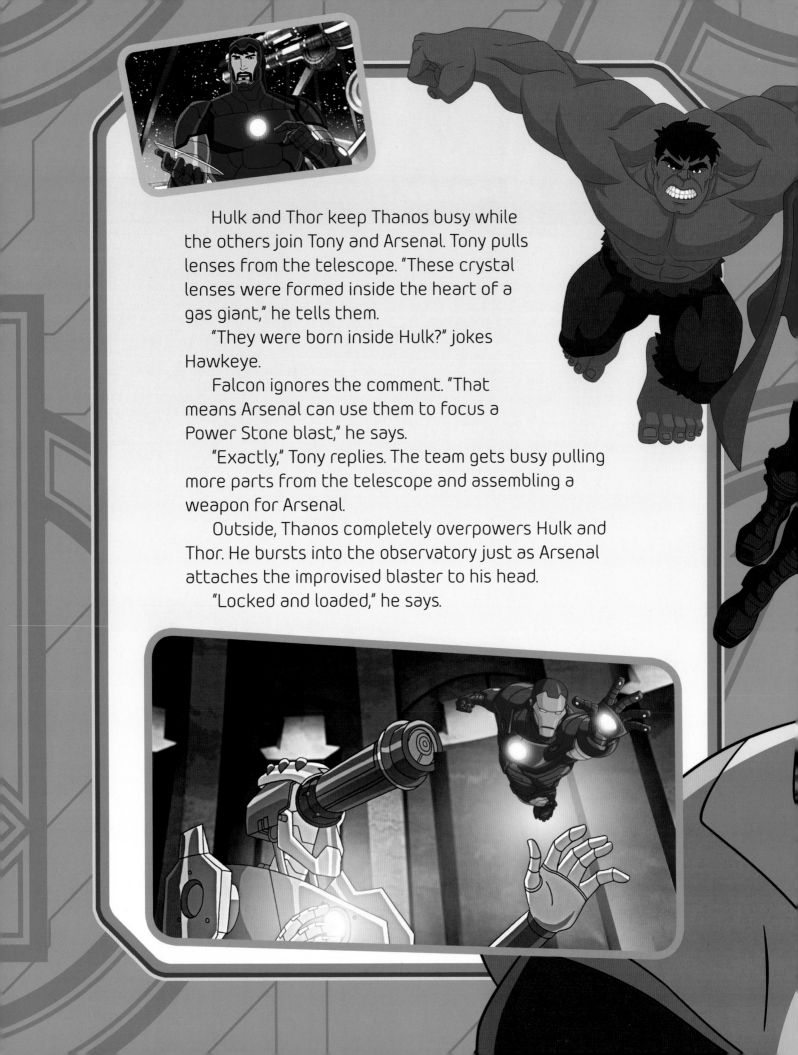

Hulk and Thor keep Thanos busy while the others join Tony and Arsenal. Tony pulls lenses from the telescope. "These crystal lenses were formed inside the heart of a gas giant," he tells them.

"They were born inside Hulk?" jokes Hawkeye.

Falcon ignores the comment. "That means Arsenal can use them to focus a Power Stone blast," he says.

"Exactly," Tony replies. The team gets busy pulling more parts from the telescope and assembling a weapon for Arsenal.

Outside, Thanos completely overpowers Hulk and Thor. He bursts into the observatory just as Arsenal attaches the improvised blaster to his head.

"Locked and loaded," he says.

BOOM! BOOM! BOOM!

Thanos stands before the Avengers. "If you're the mightiest Earth has to offer, your planet is doomed." He stomps on the floor and creates a micro-quake, knocking everybody off their feet.

Tony orders Arsenal to shoot. "Make Dad proud," he says. The robot prepares to fire.

Thanos laughs. "Your toys are meaningless to me."

"You haven't met Arsenal," says Tony. Arsenal releases the energy of the Power Stone. It refracts through the crystal lenses and shoots out in a focused bolt of energy.

The brute tries to shield himself, but the sustained blast surrounds him and explodes! Thanos is hurled into the air.

Arsenal takes off the apparatus. "Tony, I believe the mission is complete."

Iron Man is proud of his friend. "Couldn't be more complete," he says.

ZAP!

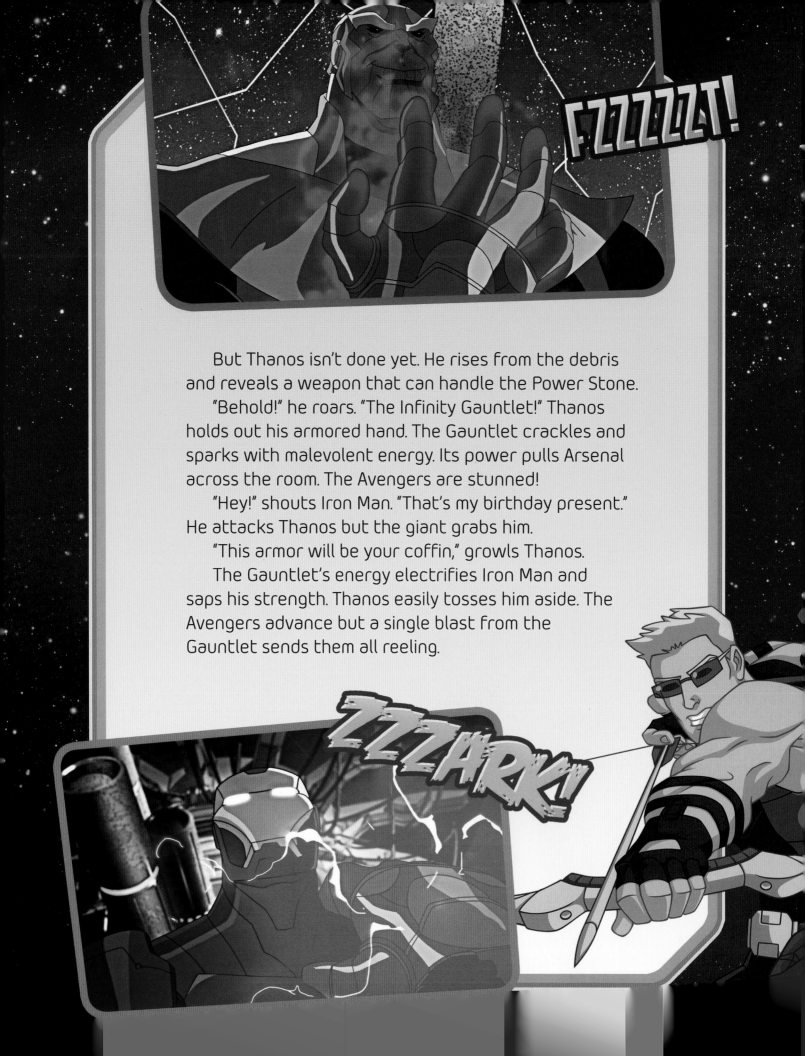

FZZZZZZT!

But Thanos isn't done yet. He rises from the debris and reveals a weapon that can handle the Power Stone.

"Behold!" he roars. "The Infinity Gauntlet!" Thanos holds out his armored hand. The Gauntlet crackles and sparks with malevolent energy. Its power pulls Arsenal across the room. The Avengers are stunned!

"Hey!" shouts Iron Man. "That's my birthday present." He attacks Thanos but the giant grabs him.

"This armor will be your coffin," growls Thanos.

The Gauntlet's energy electrifies Iron Man and saps his strength. Thanos easily tosses him aside. The Avengers advance but a single blast from the Gauntlet sends them all reeling.

ZZZZARK!

Thanos takes hold of Arsenal. The robot is powerless to resist. The immense strength of the Gauntlet draws the Power Stone out of Arsenal's chest. Its energy courses through Thanos, making him mightier than ever!

"Avengers," he thunders. "You rejected my offer. I shall not spare your world." The villain launches himself off the Moon and heads for Earth.

"Any more pages out of your bad idea playbook?" Hawkeye says with more than a touch of sarcasm.

Captain America is not amused. "We're never out of options," he says. "Falcon, check Watcher's computer. The Power Stone must have a weakness."

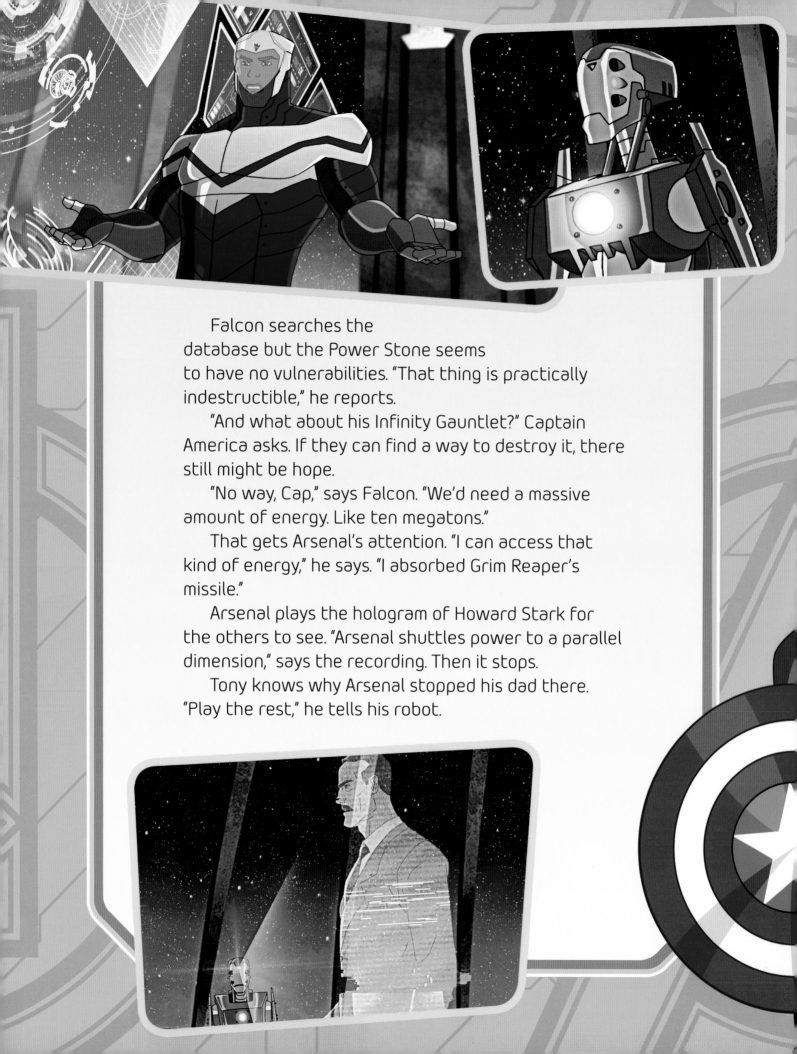

Falcon searches the database but the Power Stone seems to have no vulnerabilities. "That thing is practically indestructible," he reports.

"And what about his Infinity Gauntlet?" Captain America asks. If they can find a way to destroy it, there still might be hope.

"No way, Cap," says Falcon. "We'd need a massive amount of energy. Like ten megatons."

That gets Arsenal's attention. "I can access that kind of energy," he says. "I absorbed Grim Reaper's missile."

Arsenal plays the hologram of Howard Stark for the others to see. "Arsenal shuttles power to a parallel dimension," says the recording. Then it stops.

Tony knows why Arsenal stopped his dad there. "Play the rest," he tells his robot.

Howard Stark continues. "If he had to, Arsenal could bring the power back. But that would obliterate him."

Tony watches the image of his father fade away and turns to the Avengers. "That doesn't work for me," he says.

Black Widow doesn't see it that way. "We have to play the hand we're dealt."

Captain America agrees. Everyone knows it's not an easy decision, but Earth has to come first.

"I was created to do one thing—to protect you," Arsenal reminds Tony. "Permit me."

Tony knows they're right. "All right. Let's do this."

Falcon explains that overpowering Thanos won't be easy. "I need to get a live reading when the Power Stone is in use," he says. The Avengers will need to draw fire from the Gauntlet to accomplish the mission.

The Watcher happens to have a collection of souvenirs from Thanos's home world. "Armor battle suits! These will make him cranky," says Hawkeye.

The Avengers fly out to confront Thanos in the borrowed armor. But the suits pose little threat to him. "They didn't help the Titan army when I destroyed them," Thanos gloats.

"This time, you're fighting the Avengers," responds Captain America. He throws his shield, but Thanos blasts it away from him.

Hulk hurls a massive fist at Thanos. The punch is blocked! Thor and his mighty hammer land a solid blow. Thanos shakes it off. Hawkeye fires missile after missile but they do no harm. Even so, the Avengers' plan is working. Thanos fires the Power Stone weapon over and over again.

"I got it!" says Falcon from the Avengers' ship. "Eighty-seven tera-hertz. Arsenal, adjust your energy output to that frequency."

"Understood," says the robot.

Captain America and the others continue to battle Thanos, keeping him busy while Arsenal gets into position. As soon as he's ready, the robot begins drawing back megatons of stored power.

ZAP!

Iron Man fires on Thanos. The shots give Arsenal the time he needs.

"Why do you waste my time with your futile efforts?" Thanos sneers.

"You say futile, I say genius!" replies Iron Man, blasting him again. Suddenly, the other Avengers fly off in retreat.

"Ha, ha! Even your friends are abandoning you," laughs Thanos. "They fear true power."

"You're wrong," says Iron Man. "My friends are my true power!"

At that very second, Arsenal's massive sphere of energy engulfs Thanos.

"Good-bye, Tony," says the robot.

Thanos realizes he's trapped. "What?" he mutters. BOOM!

KA-BOOM!

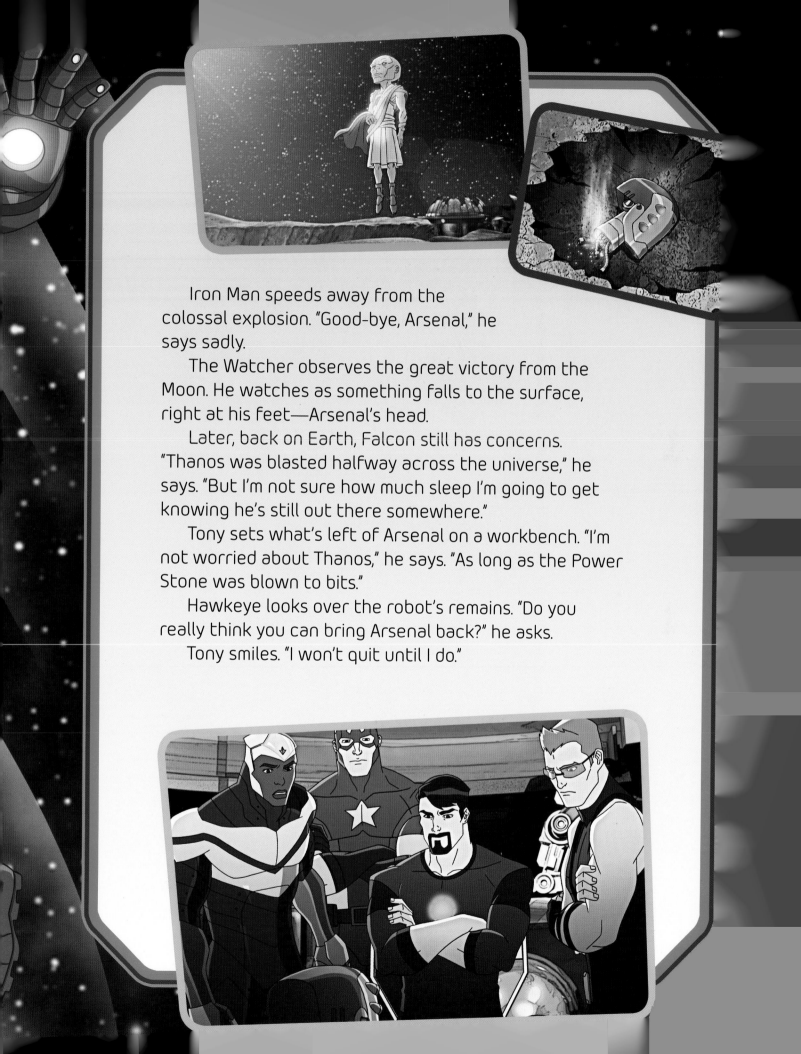

Iron Man speeds away from the colossal explosion. "Good-bye, Arsenal," he says sadly.

The Watcher observes the great victory from the Moon. He watches as something falls to the surface, right at his feet—Arsenal's head.

Later, back on Earth, Falcon still has concerns. "Thanos was blasted halfway across the universe," he says. "But I'm not sure how much sleep I'm going to get knowing he's still out there somewhere."

Tony sets what's left of Arsenal on a workbench. "I'm not worried about Thanos," he says. "As long as the Power Stone was blown to bits."

Hawkeye looks over the robot's remains. "Do you really think you can bring Arsenal back?" he asks.

Tony smiles. "I won't quit until I do."

BUILDING INSTRUCTIONS

When building your models, press out only the pieces needed for each step as shown in the white boxes. The dotted lines on the pieces are guides for folding. All the pieces have numbered tabs and/or slots. When assembling the models, match the numbers on the tabs and slots to connect the pieces.

IRON MAN

HEAD

Press out this piece.

head

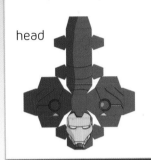

Follow the fold lines to create Iron Man's head as shown below.

Match the tab and slot numbers to close the box.

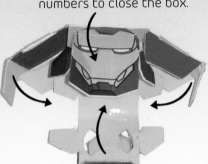

The head should look like this when you are finished folding.

BODY

Fold Iron Man's chest armor and abdomen pieces as shown. Remember to use the numbers on the tabs and slots as a guide.

Press out these pieces.

A. chest armor

B. abdomen

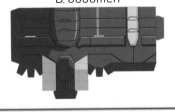

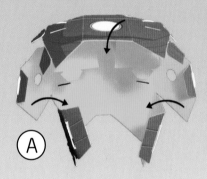

Ⓐ

Ⓑ

To assemble the upper body, slide part B up and into part A.

Ⓐ

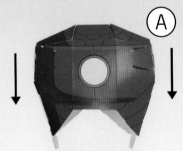

Ⓑ

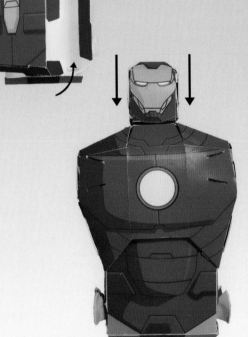

You now have Iron Man's body. Attach the head to the top of the chest as shown by sliding the tabs on the head into the slots in the chest.

ARMS

Both of Iron Man's arms are folded and constructed the same way. For each arm, make sure you are using the correct pieces. They are different. Assemble one arm at a time.

Fold pieces A, B, C, and D as shown. To assemble the arm, line up the holes in the tabs at the elbow.

Press out these pieces.

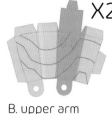

A. lower arm (right and left)

B. upper arm (right and left)

C. elbow pad X2

D. shoulder pad X2

Carefully slide the elbow pad connectors into the holes in the elbow joint.

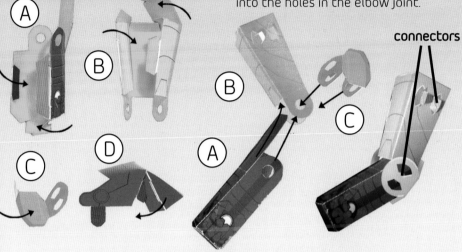

connectors

Use the number guides on the upper arm connectors and the circular holes on Iron Man's shoulders to attach the arms. Finally, attach the shoulder pads by matching the numbers on the tabs and slots.

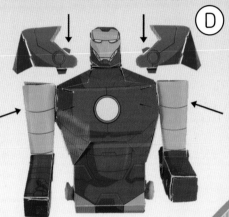

TIP: Each connector in all the models must be opened up inside the arm/leg for a secure connection. It is helpful to use the back of a pencil to reach it.

LEGS

The legs are assembled the same way as the arms. Assemble one leg at a time.

Press out these pieces.

A. upper leg (right and left)

X2

B. lower leg (right and left)

X2

C. knee pad

X2

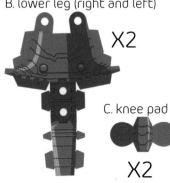

Fold pieces A, B, and C as shown.

To assemble the leg, line up the holes in the tabs at the knee. Carefully slide the knee pad connectors into the holes in the knee joint.

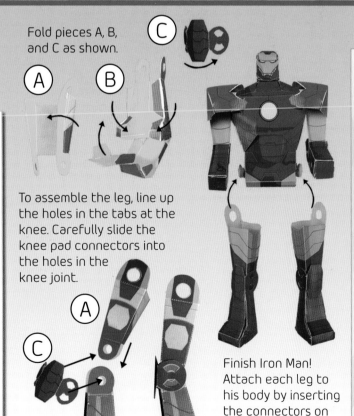

Finish Iron Man! Attach each leg to his body by inserting the connectors on the torso into the holes in the tabs on his upper legs.

YOU BUILT IRON MAN!

CAPTAIN AMERICA

HEaD

Follow the fold lines to create Captain America's head as shown.

Press out this piece.

head

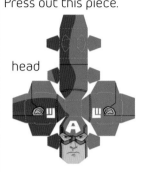

Match the tab and slot numbers to close the box.

The head should look like this when you are finished folding.

BODY

Captain America's body is one big piece. Fold as shown. Remember to use the numbers on the tabs and slots as a guide.

Press out this piece.

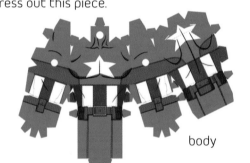

body

You now have Captain America's body. Attach the head to the top of the chest as shown by sliding the tabs on the head into the slots in the chest.

RIGHT ARM

Captain America's right arm carries his shield. Make sure you are using the correct arm pieces. They are different than the left arm.

Press out these pieces.

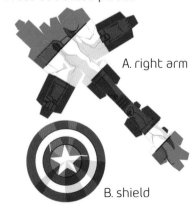

A. right arm

B. shield

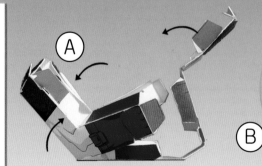

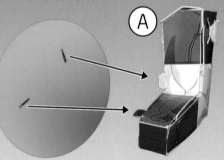

Carefully fold the arm as shown and insert the tabs into the matching numbered slots.

Attach the shield to the folded arm by sliding the tabs on the arm into the matching slots in the shield, using the numbers on the slots and tabs as a guide.

LEFT ARM

Captain America's left arm is assembled the same way as Iron Man's.

Fold pieces A, B, and C as shown.

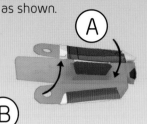

To assemble the arm, line up the holes in the tabs at the elbow.

Press out these pieces.

A. left lower arm   B. left upper arm

C. elbow pad

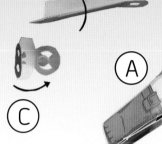

Carefully slide the elbow pad connectors into the holes in the elbow joint.

Use the number guides on the upper arm connectors and the circular holes in Captain America's shoulders to attach the arms.

LEGS

The legs are assembled the same way as Iron Man's. Assemble one leg at a time.

Fold pieces A, B, and C as shown.

Press out these pieces.

A. upper leg (right and left)

X2

X2

B. lower leg (right and left)

X2

C. knee pad

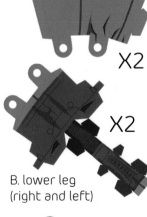

To assemble the leg, line up the holes in the tabs at the knee. Carefully slide the knee pad connectors into the holes in the knee joint.

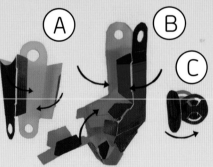

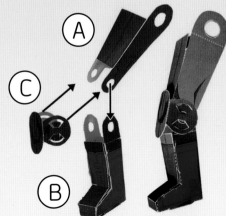

Give the Captain his legs! Attach each leg to his body by inserting the connectors on the torso into the holes in the tabs on his upper legs.

YOU BUILT CAPTAIN AMERICA!

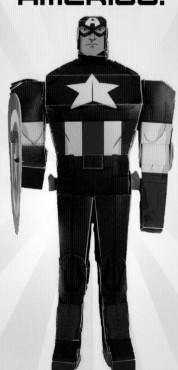

THE HULK

HEAD

Fold the head as shown.

Press out this piece.

head

The head should look like this when you are finished folding.

BODY

Fold the body as shown and attach the head by lining up the tabs and slots.

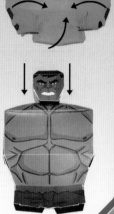

Press out this piece.

body

ARMS

Fold each arm and attach it to the body with the connector. Make sure you put the arms on the correct sides of the body!

Press out these pieces.

arm (right and left)

X2

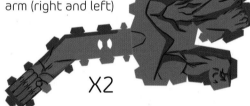

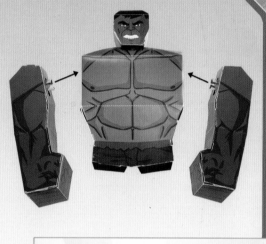

YOU BUILT THE HULK!

NOW THE AVENGERS CAN ASSEMBLE!

LEGS

Fold each leg and attach it to the body with the tabs. Make sure each leg is attached to the correct side of the body. Use the numbers as a guide!

Press out these pieces.

leg (right and left)

X2

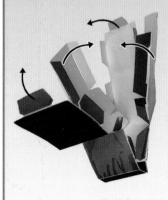

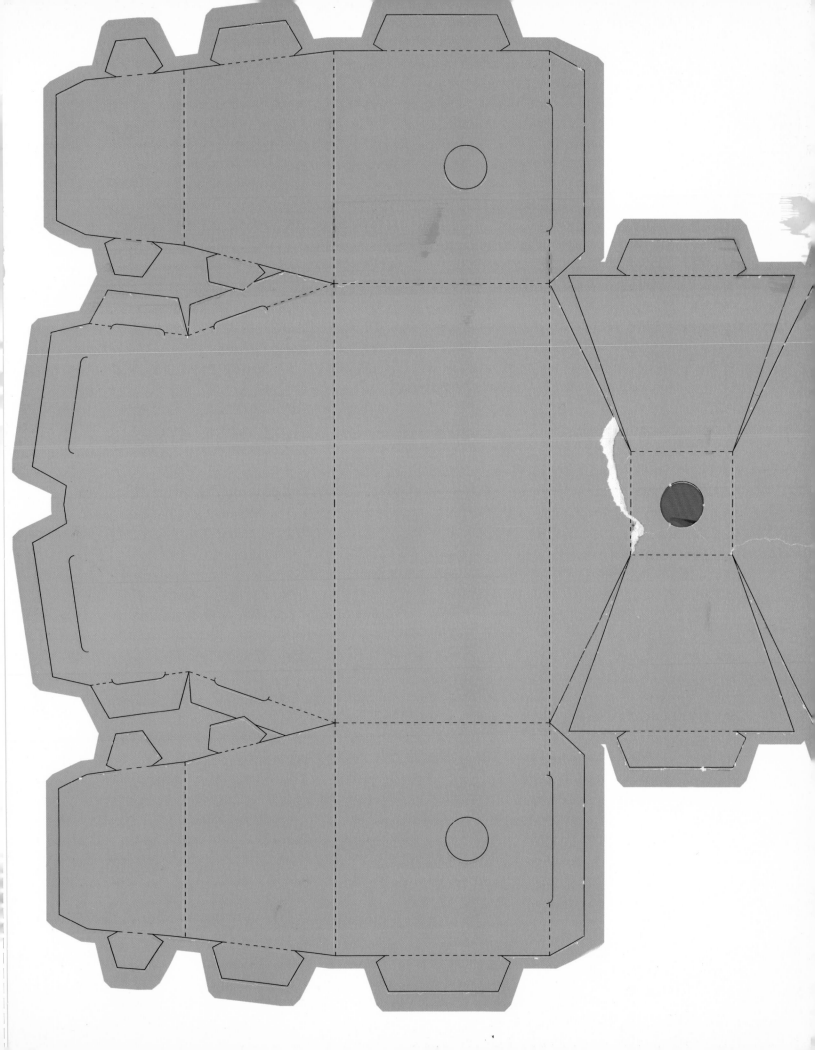

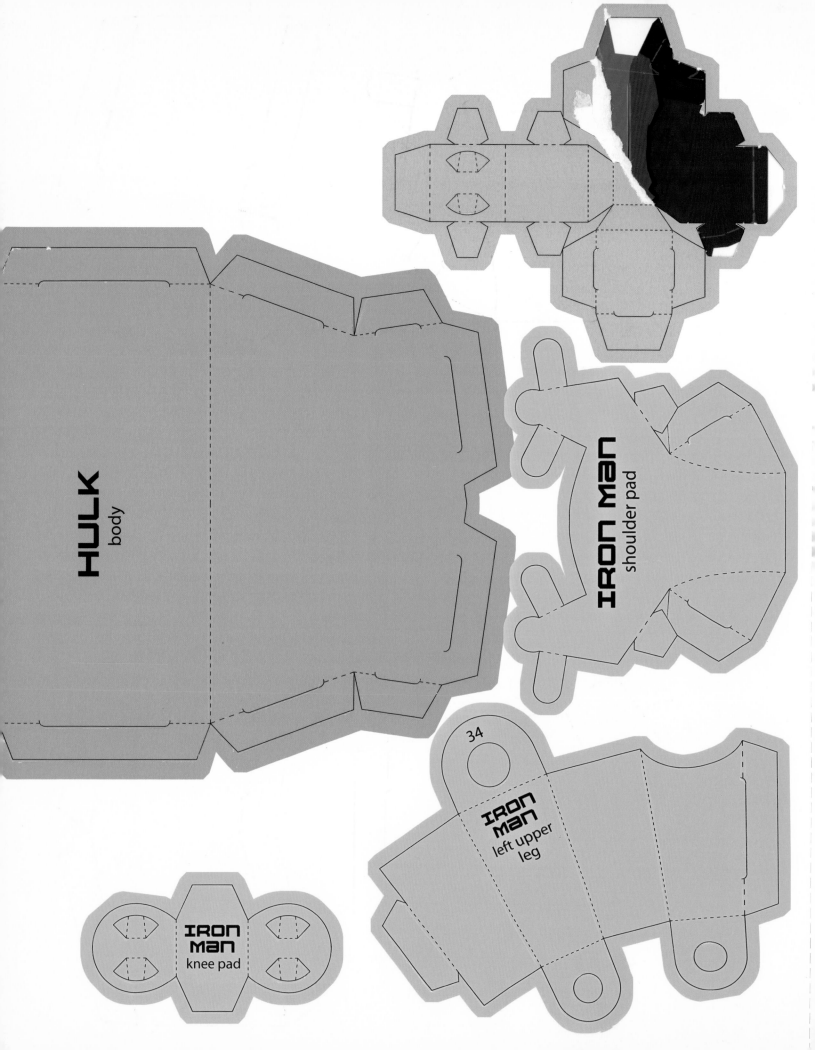

HULK
body

IRON MAN
shoulder pad

34

IRON MAN
left upper
leg

IRON MAN
knee pad

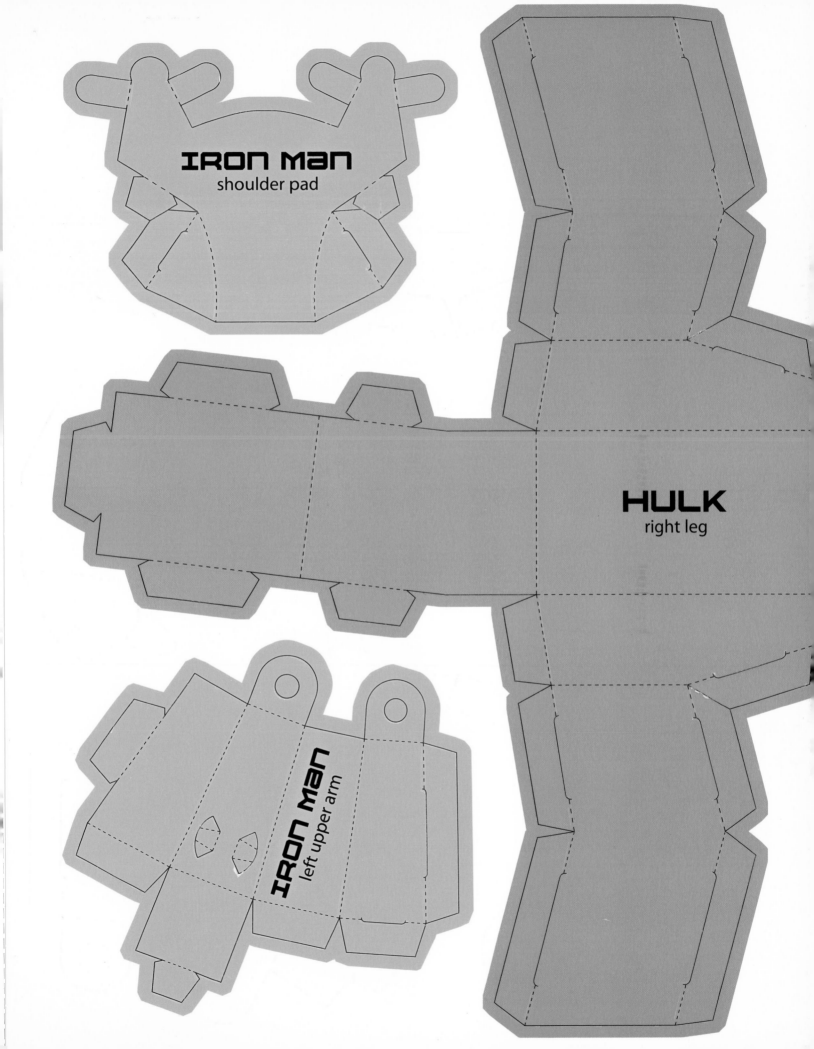

IRON MAN
shoulder pad

HULK
right leg

IRON MAN
left upper arm

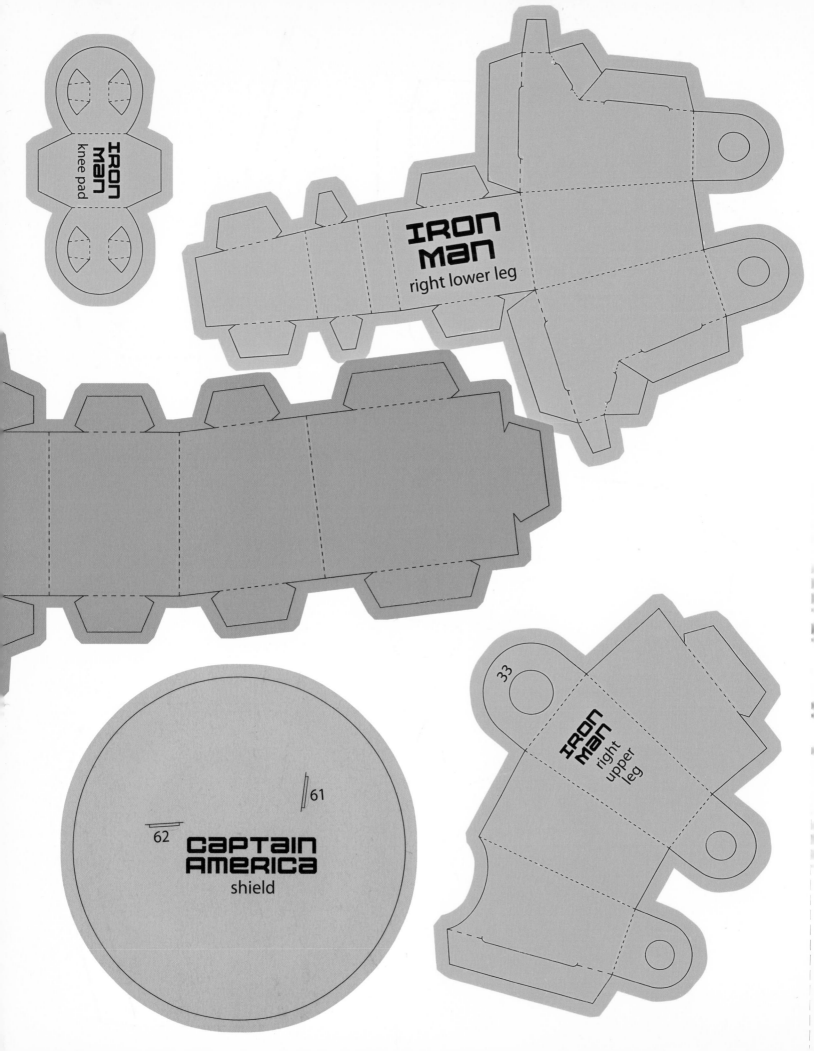

IRON
MAN
knee pad

IRON
MAN
right lower leg

CAPTAIN
AMERICA
shield

62

61

IRON
MAN
right
upper
leg

33

IRON MAN
right upper arm

HULK
left leg

CAPTAIN AMERICA
right upper leg

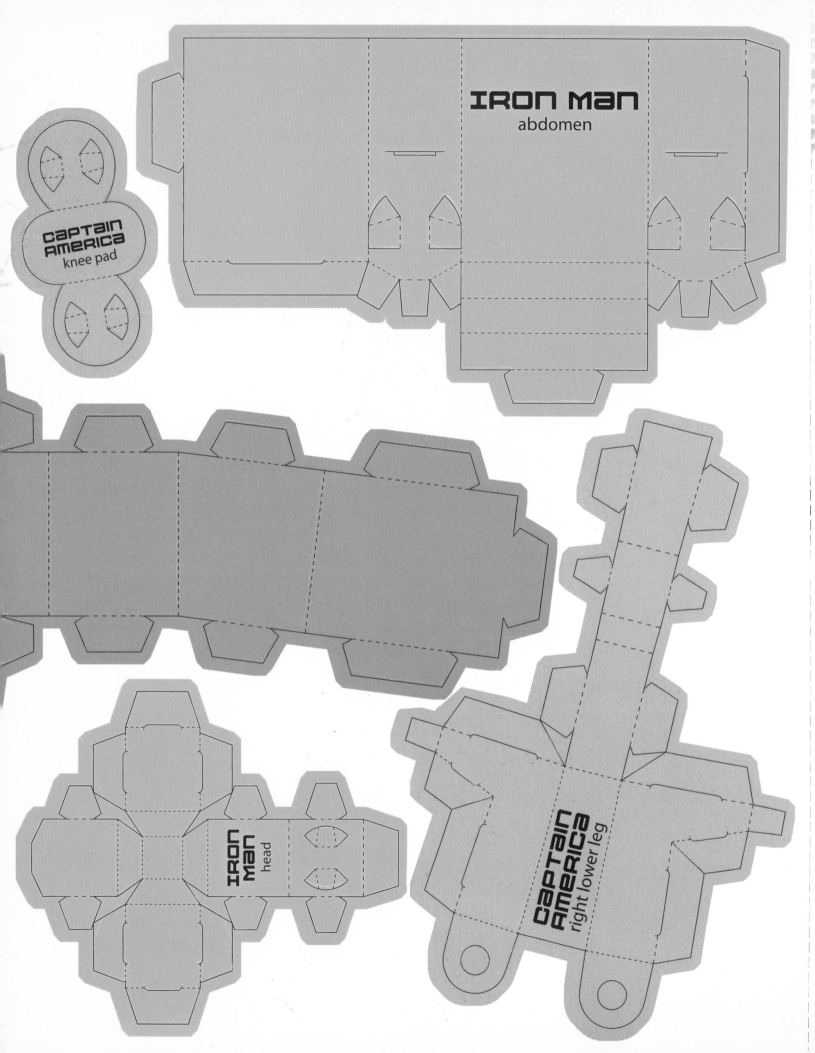

IRON MAN
abdomen

CAPTAIN
AMERICA
knee pad

IRON
MAN
head

CAPTAIN
AMERICA
right lower leg

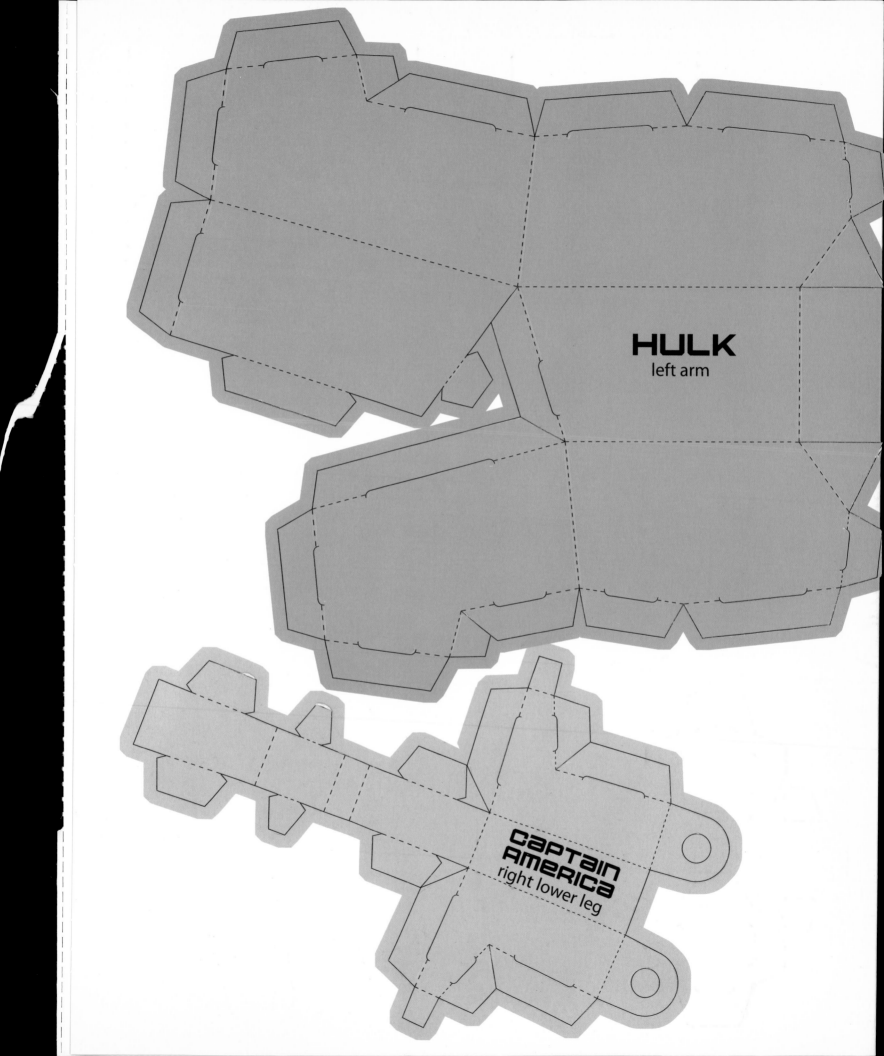

HULK
left arm

CAPTAIN
AMERICA
right lower leg

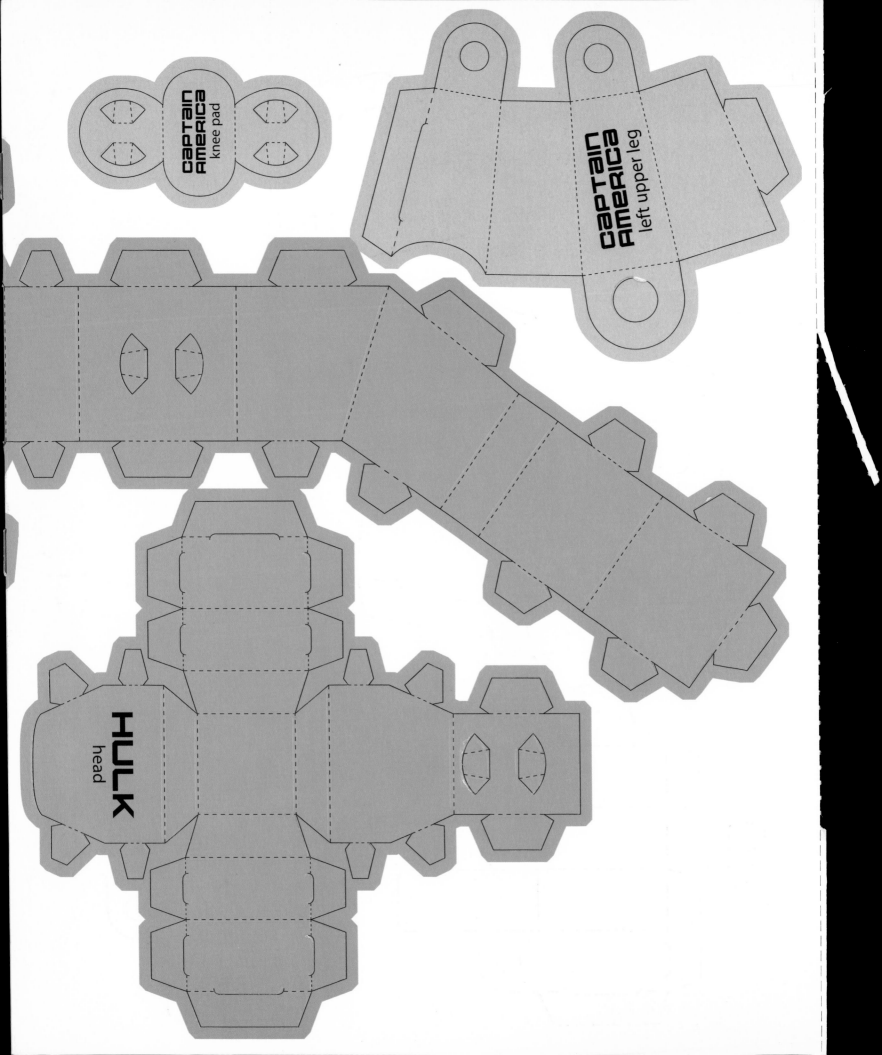

captain
AMERICA
knee pad

captain
AMERICA
left upper leg

HULK
head

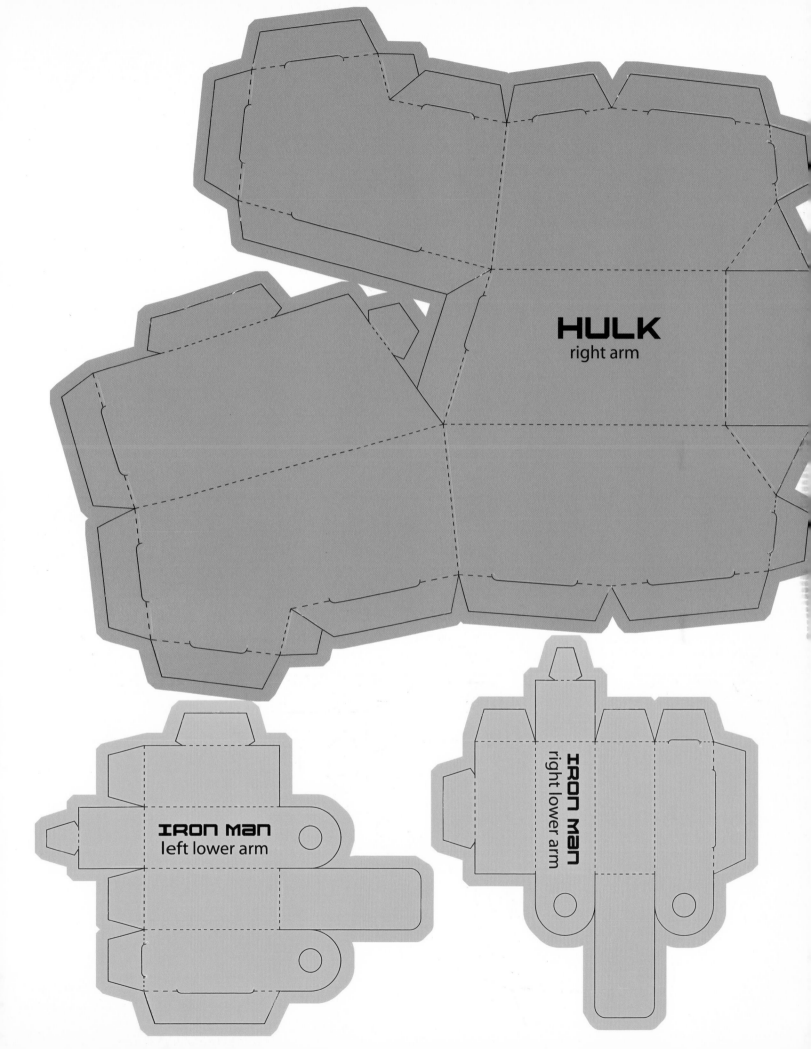

HULK
right arm

IRON MAN
left lower arm

IRON MAN
right lower arm

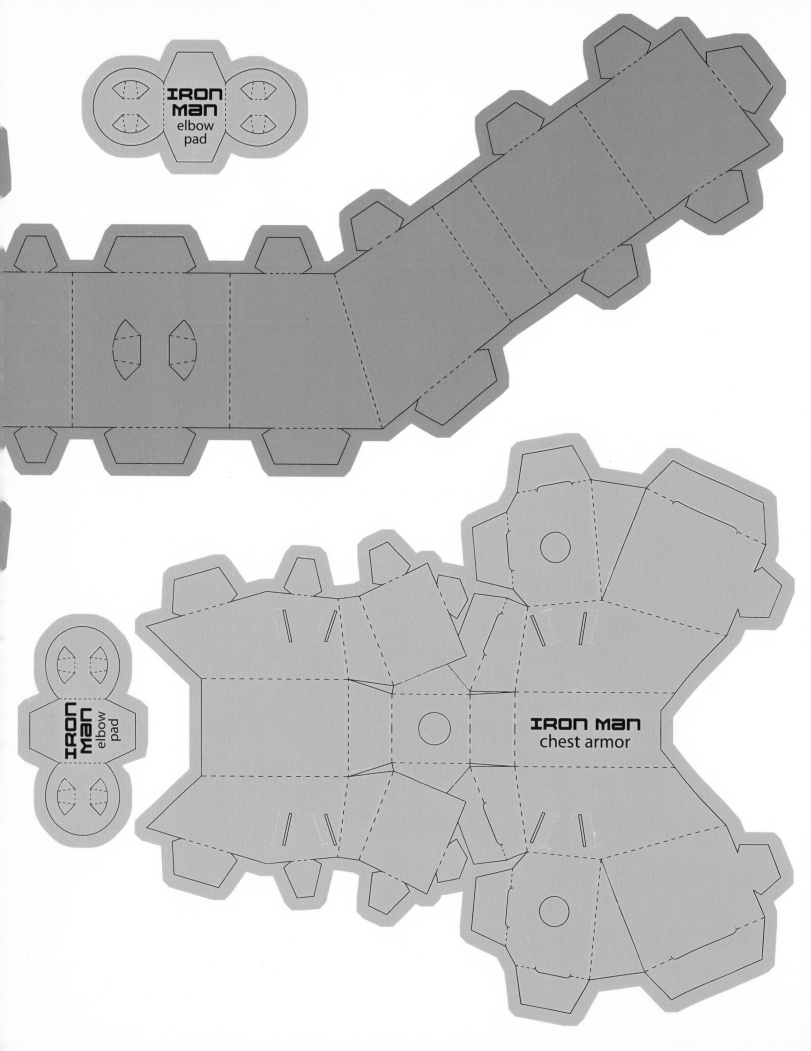

IRON
MAN
elbow
pad

IRON
MAN
elbow
pad

IRON MAN
chest armor

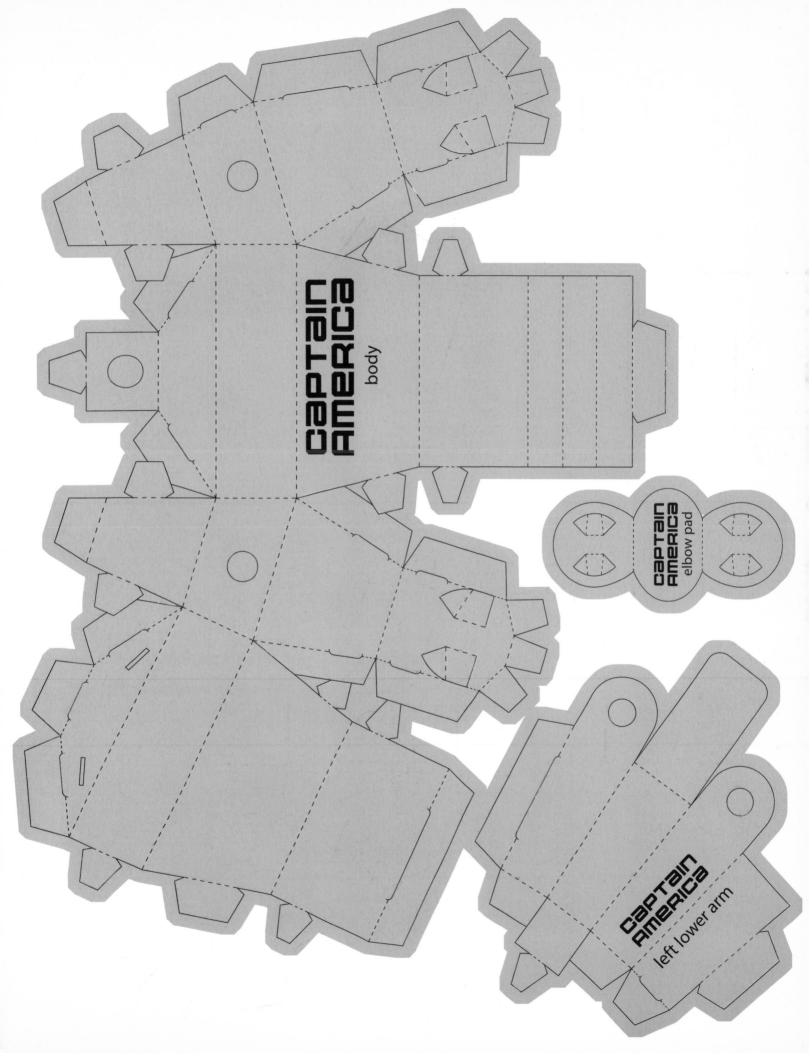

CAPTAIN AMERICA
body

CAPTAIN AMERICA
elbow pad

CAPTAIN AMERICA
left lower arm

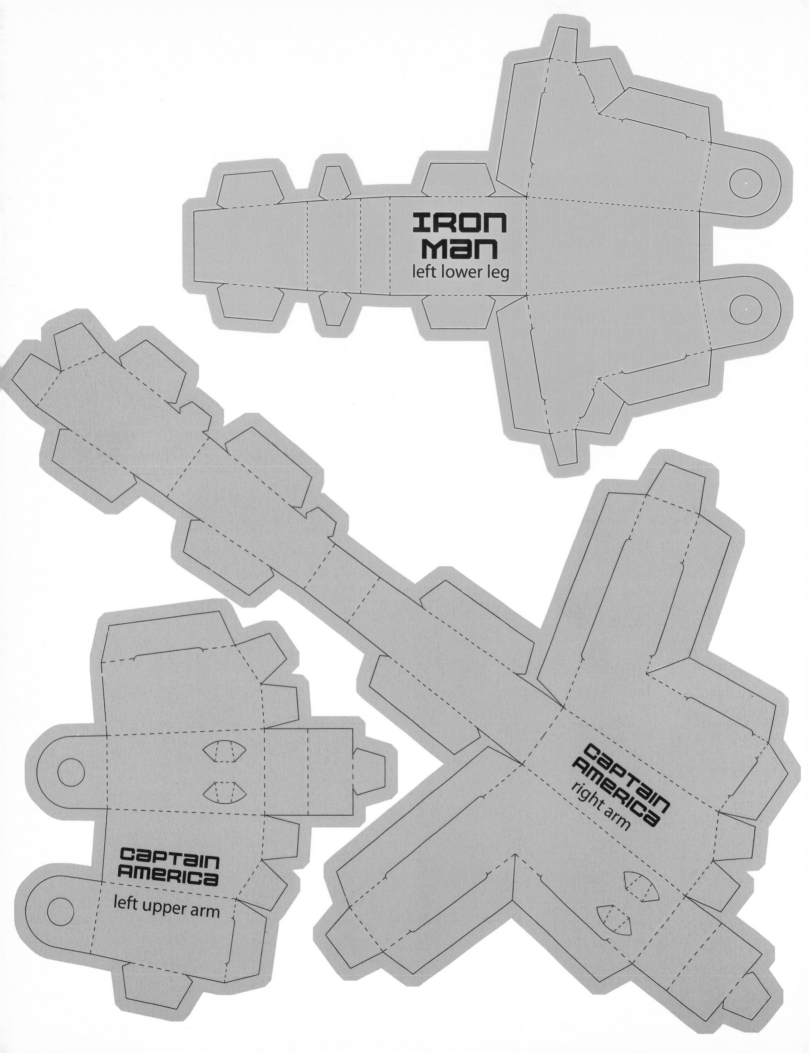

IRON
MAN
left lower leg

CAPTAIN
AMERICA
right arm

CAPTAIN
AMERICA
left upper arm